LOTS MORE
FARMYARD TALES

Heather Amery

Illustrated by Stephen Cartwright

Edited by Jenny Tyler

Language consultant: Betty Root

There is a little yellow duck to

Notes for Parents

The stories in this delightful picture book are ones which your child will want to share with you many times.

All the stories in *Farmyard Tales* have been written in a special way to ensure that young children succeed in their first efforts to read.

To help with that success, first read the whole of one story aloud and talk about the pictures. Then encourage your child to read the short, simpler text at the top of each page and read the longer text at the bottom of the page yourself. This "turn about" reading builds up confidence and children do love joining in. It is a great day when they discover that they can read a whole story for themselves.

Farmyard Tales provides an enjoyable opportunity for parents and children to share the excitement of learning to read.

Betty Root

THE SNOW STORM

This is Apple Tree Farm.

This is Mrs. Boot, the farmer. She has two children called Poppy and Sam, and a dog called Rusty.

In the night there was a big snow storm.

In the morning, it is still snowing. "You must wrap up warm," says Mrs. Boot to Poppy and Sam.

Ted works on the farm.

He helps Mrs. Boot look after the animals.
He gives them food and water every day.

“Come and help me,” calls Ted.

“Where are you going?” says Poppy.
“I’m taking this hay to the sheep,” says Ted.

Poppy and Sam pull the hay.

They go out of the farmyard with Ted.
They walk to the gate of the sheep field.

“Where are the sheep?” says Sam.

“They are all covered with snow,” says Ted.
“We’ll have to find them,” says Poppy.

They brush the snow off the sheep.

Ted, Poppy and Sam give each sheep lots of hay.
"They've got nice warm coats," says Sam.

Poppy counts the sheep.

"There are only six sheep. One is missing," says Poppy. "It's that naughty Woolly," saysTed.

They look for Woolly.

They walk around the snowy field.
"Rusty, good dog, find Woolly," calls Sam.

Rusty runs across the field.

Ted, Poppy and Sam run after him. Rusty barks at the thick hedge.

Ted looks under the hedge.

"Can you see anything?" says Sam. "Yes, Woolly is hiding in there. Clever Rusty," says Ted.

“Come on, Woolly.”

“Let me help you out, old girl,” says Ted. Carefully he pulls Woolly out of the hedge.

"There's something else!"

"Look, I can see something moving," says Sam.
"What is it, Ted?" says Poppy.

Ted lifts out a tiny lamb.

"Woolly has had a lamb," he says. "We'll take it and Woolly to the barn. They'll be warm there."

Poppy rides home.

She holds the lamb. “What a surprise!” she says. “Good old Woolly.”

SURPRISE VISITORS

This is Apple Tree Farm.

This is Mrs. Boot, the farmer. She has two children called Poppy and Sam, and a dog called Rusty.

Today is Saturday.

Mrs. Boot, Poppy and Sam are having breakfast.
"Why are the cows so noisy?" asks Sam.

They all run out to the field.

The cows are running around the field. They are scared. A big balloon is floating over the trees.

“It’s a hot air balloon.”

“It’s coming down,” says Mrs. Boot. “It’s going to land in our field.” The balloon hits the ground.

There are two people in it.

"Where are we?" asks the man. "This is Apple Tree Farm. You frightened our cows," says Mrs. Boot.

The man climbs out.

“I’m Alice and this is Tim,” says the woman.
“We ran out of gas. Sorry about your cows.”

"A truck is following us."

"There it is now," says Alice. "Our friend is bringing more cylinders of gas for the balloon."

Alice helps to unload the truck.

Tim unloads the empty cylinders. Then he puts the new ones into the balloon's basket.

They blow up the balloon.

Poppy and Sam help Tim hold open the balloon. A fan blows hot air into it. It gets bigger and bigger.

"Would you like a ride?"

"Oh, yes please," says Poppy. "Just a little one," says Tim. "The truck will bring you back."

Mrs. Boot, Poppy and Sam climb in.

Tim lights the gas burner. The big flames make a loud noise. "Hold on tight," says Alice.

The balloon goes up.

Slowly it leaves the ground. Tim turns off the burner. “The wind is blowing us along,” he says.

The balloon floats along.

“I can see our farm down there,” says Poppy.
“Look, there’s Alice in the truck,” says Sam.

"We're going down now," says Tim.

The balloon floats down and the basket lands in a field. Mrs. Boot helps Poppy and Sam out.

“Thank you very much.”

They wave as the balloon takes off again.
“We were flying,” says Sam.

MARKET DAY

This is Apple Tree Farm.

This is Mrs. Boot, the farmer. She has two children called Poppy and Sam, and a dog called Rusty.

Today is market day.

Mrs. Boot puts the trailer on the car.
Poppy and Sam put a wire crate in the trailer.

They drive to the market.

Mrs. Boot, Poppy and Sam walk past cows, sheep and pigs. They go to the shed which has cages of birds.

There are different kinds of geese.

“Let’s look in all the cages,” says Mrs. Boot.
“I want four nice young geese.”

"There are four nice white ones."

"They look nice and friendly," says Poppy.
"Yes, they are just what I want," says Mrs. Boot.

A woman is selling the geese.

“How much are the four white ones?” asks Mrs. Boot. “I’ll buy them, please.” She pays for them.

"We'll come back later."

"Let's look at the other birds," says Sam. There are cages with hens, chicks, ducks and pigeons.

"Look at the poor little duck."

"It's lonely," says Poppy. "Please may I buy it? I can pay for it with my own money."

“Yes, you can buy it.”

“We’ll get it when we come back for the geese,” says Mrs. Boot. Poppy pays the man for the duck.

Mrs. Boot brings the crate.

Poppy opens the lid. The woman passes the geese to Mrs. Boot. She puts them in the crate.

One of the geese runs away.

A goose jumps out of the crate just before Sam shuts the door. It runs very fast out of the shed.

“Catch that goose.”

Mrs. Boot, Poppy and Sam run after the goose.
The goose jumps through an open car door.

"Now we've got it," says Sam.

But a woman opens a door on the other side.
The goose jumps out of the car and runs away.

"Run after it," says Mrs. Boot.

The goose runs into the plant tent.
"There it is," says Sam, and picks it up.

“Let’s go home,” says Mrs. Boot.

“I’ve got my geese now.” “And I’ve got my duck,” says Poppy. “Markets are fun,” says Sam.

CAMPING OUT

This is Apple Tree Farm.

This is Mrs. Boot, the farmer. She has two children called Poppy and Sam, and a dog called Rusty.

A car stops at the gate.

A man, a woman and a boy get out. “Hello,” says the man. “May we camp on your farm?”

“Yes, you can camp over there.”

“We’ll show you the way,” says Mr. Boot.
The campers follow in their car.

The campers put up their tent.

Poppy and Sam help them. They take chairs, a table, a cooking stove and food out of the car.

Then they all go to the farmhouse.

Mrs. Boot gives the campers a bucket of water and some milk. Poppy and Sam bring some eggs.

"Can we go camping?"

"Please, Dad, can we put our tent up too?" says Poppy. "Oh yes, please Dad," says Sam.

Mr. Boot gets out the tent.

Poppy and Sam try to put up the little blue tent but it keeps falling down. At last it is ready.

“Come and have supper.”

“Then you can go to the tent,” says Mrs. Boot.
“But you must wash and brush your teeth first.”

Poppy and Sam go to the tent.

"It's not dark yet," says Sam. "Come on, Rusty. You can come camping with us," says Poppy.

Poppy and Sam go to bed.

They crawl into the tent and tie up the door.
Then they wriggle into their sleeping bags.

"What's that noise?"

Sam sits up. "There's something walking around outside the tent," says Sam. "What is it?"

Poppy looks out of the tent.

"It's only old Daisy, the cow," she says. "She must have strayed into this field. She's so nosy."

Daisy looks into the tent.

Rusty barks at her. Daisy is scared. She tries to back away but the tent catches on her head.

Daisy pulls at the tent.

She pulls it down and runs off with it. Rusty chases her. Poppy and Sam run back to the house.

Mr. Boot opens the door.

"Hello, Dad," says Sam. "Daisy's got our tent."
"I don't like camping after all," says Poppy.

First published in 1995 by Usborne Publishing Ltd, Usborne House, 83-85 Saffron Hill, London EC1N 8RT
Printed in Italy. First published in America August 1995. UE.